THE LOST DIARY OF
ANNIE OAKLEY'S
WILD WEST STAGEHAND

THE LOST DIARY OF
ANNIE OAKLEY'S
WILD WEST STAGEHAND

LASSOED BY CLIVE DICKINSON

Illustrated by George Hollingworth

An imprint of HarperCollins*Publishers*

First published in Great Britain by Collins in 2001

Collins is an imprint of HarperCollins*Publishers* Ltd
77-85 Fulham Palace Road, Hammersmith,
London, W6 8JB

The HarperCollins website address is
www.fireandwater.com

Text copyright © Clive Dickinson 2001
Illustrations by George Hollingworth 2001
Cover illustration by Martin Chatterton 2001

ISBN 978 0 00 694597 0

The author and illustrators assert the moral right to be
identified as the author and illustrators of the work.

MESSAGE TO READERS

What do you do when you unexpectedly find a previously unknown document about a famous person? Sell it to a newspaper? Sell it to a television company? Put it back where you found it? Tear it up as bedding for your gerbils?

This was exactly the difficulty faced by Clive Dickinson during a visit to Germany. While he was unwrapping a cuckoo clock he had bought, he discovered what looked like a very thick exercise book lining the bottom of the box. Inside were pages and pages of writing, not in German, as he might have expected, but in English.

To make sure he wasn't going cuckoo himself, Mr Dickinson flicked through the pages and found dates from the 1880s, which suggested that the book was a kind of journal. All the way through, he spotted the name of Annie Oakley, who was one of the most famous American women in the world one hundred years ago.

Before going public, Mr Dickinson asked for professional help. In exchange for return flights to Europe, all expenses paid, two experts on the American West, Professor Joe King of Larfinstock College and Dr Rusty Brayne of Imina State University, confirmed that he had made a unique find. In their experience, nothing quite like it had ever been discovered before.

After careful study, lasting two weeks in an expensive hotel, they agreed that the book lining the box of the cuckoo clock was the personal diary of one Phil McCartridge. He seems to have worked as Annie Oakley's stagehand during the years in which she became world famous for her amazing shooting act in the show called Buffalo Bill's Wild West.

Working closely with Annie Oakley, Phil McCartridge was able to record day-to-day details about her and her friends: the cowboys, Native American Indians, animal-handlers, stable-hands and riders, who helped recreate life in the Wild West for spectators on both sides of the Atlantic.

Now this remarkable document can be published for the first time, bringing alive the thrills and skills, dangers and excitements which Buffalo Bill's Wild West brought to millions of people in America and Europe a century and more ago.

24 APRIL 1885 – LOUISVILLE, KENTUCKY

Well, I'll be...!

I thought I'd seen just about all there was to see about guns and shooting and the Wild West. But not after today. No, sir.

Colt, Remington, Lancaster, Winchester, Double Gloucester – there ain't a gun this side of the Rocky Mountains that I don't know. And there ain't a champion sharp-shooter I ain't seen – leastways, not till this afternoon.

Now, I may not be that quick at book learning, but I know a sure bet when I see one. I reckon I could be on to a good thing if I start writing down what goes on around here. I can see my name in print already on one of those fancy book covers and in the newspapers.

TEXAS TORNADO
PHIL McCARTRIDGE BLOWS YOU AWAY
Phil McCartridge EXPLODES OFF THE PAGE

Things ain't going to be the same – that's for sure. And about time, too. Last winter was the worst this show has ever known. First the steamship carrying everything down the river ran into another steamship and sank. We lost animals, wagons and camp gear, not to mention my precious guns and ammunition. That meant the show opened late in New Orleans, which ain't good for business, especially at Christmas.

Then it started raining. It rained and it rained until I thought the old man river* was flowing right through the camp. Only a handful of people came to watch the show. Business was so bad that Captain Bogardus, the top trick shooter on the bill, upped sticks last month and left the show for good, taking his four shooting sons with him. With our top gun gone, we didn't have many shots left in the locker.

* the river Mississippi

Then Buffalo Bill told me yesterday that he's hired some sharp-shooter called Andy Oakley to take Captain Bogardus's place. I sure hoped this guy would hit the target – the show needed all the help it could get. Only the Andy Oakley who turned up today ain't what I was expecting at all. No, sir!

For one thing, Andy ain't no Andy. She's an *Annie*! And she's so dainty and so ladylike, I still can't make out how she can shoot a gun like she does. But boy (I guess I mean "girl"), can she shoot! Buffalo Bill sure knows how to pull something out of his hat when the chips are down.

There goes the cook's bell for our dinner. I'd better stop writing now, 'cos I'm going to wash my hands and face for this meal – and that's something I ain't done for a very long time.

25 APRIL 1885 – LOUISVILLE, KENTUCKY

Yesterday was our first day in town, so everyone was busy getting ready for the street parade before the afternoon performance. We only do the street parade on the first day, so this morning I've got time to carry on from where I left off.

Nate Salsbury was getting real excited about Miss Oakley yesterday. Mr Salsbury is the business manager and he don't get carried away like Buffalo Bill does sometimes.

Most of us were at the street parade in town when Annie and her husband, Frank Butler, arrived in camp. Mr Salsbury watched her practising her shooting in the arena and he liked what he saw! She shot clay pigeons as they whizzed from the trap, holding her gun right side up, upside down, in her left hand and in her right. He said those clay pigeons came flying straight one after the other, and she didn't miss a single one.

Right there he signed her up to join the show – without even talking it over with Buffalo Bill. Here's another incredible thing – Mr Salsbury ordered $7,000 worth of posters of Annie before they even had a business agreement! I sure hope he knows what he's doing.

When we got back from the parade, he lined us all up to meet Annie and Frank. Buffalo Bill didn't need any convincing. He swept off his hat and bowed to her with his long hair flopping over his shoulders. He then welcomed her as "Missie", which she kind of liked, I think.

Annie walked down the line, shaking hands and nodding hello to everyone in a way that was so open and kind. You could see that the cowboys, the Mexicans, the Indians, the mule-drivers, the buffalo-handlers and everyone else in the show liked her too.

That's what folks who ain't seen Buffalo Bill's Wild West don't understand. This ain't no circus, with sideshows and clowns and animals doing dumb things they've been taught to do.

Everything in the Wild West show comes straight from the real Wild West. It's just like the posters say!

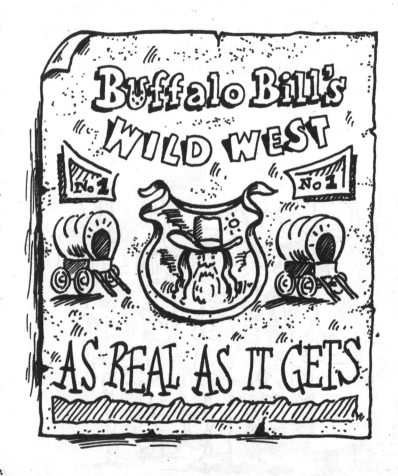

It seems to me that that's why Annie and Frank wanted to join the show. They've worked in the circus and in theatres doing trick shooting, but so have too many other so-called sharp-shooters.

Annie's been there, shot that. Now she wants folks to see how good her shooting really is. If you ask me, she couldn't have come at a better time.

26 APRIL 1885 – ON THE TRAIN

Goodbye Louisville, it's been nice seeing you – but it's even nicer having time for a real good talk with Annie and Frank, seeing as how I'm going to be looking after Annie and her guns from now on.

She's so excited, you'd think she was a little girl on her first trip away from home. Come to think of it, that's just what she looks like.

Frank's kind of quiet. He stays in the background and lets Annie do the talking, but they're a good team. Folks say he's a crack shot too. In fact he and Annie met at a shooting match. Frank was an unbeaten champion then, and Annie was just Annie Moses from a small town called Greenville, in Darke County, Ohio. But folks there reckoned Annie "could shoot a little", and she won that match fair and square.

Frank Butler was a beaten man in more ways than one that day. It wasn't long before they were married and started appearing in a shooting act called Butler and Oakley.

Why Oakley? Annie says she liked the name and it sounded good. You can't argue with that, and I've a hunch that some day the name Annie Oakley's going to be famous everywhere.

Annie ain't had an easy life, that's for sure. She started shooting when she was just a little girl, so the family could have enough to eat. Soon she was selling the game she shot and earning good money.

Owners of fancy hotels liked her game, because
there was never any gunshot in the meat. Annie
was so accurate, she always killed the birds stone
dead with a shot clean through the head.

Before long, she'd earned enough money to
repay the loan on the family farm. Since she was a
little girl, Annie ain't never had a dollar she ain't
earned herself.

She's had to work for those dollars, mind.
Travelling from town to town with Frank,
performing in music halls or circuses, staying in
cheap hotels. That's a hard way to make a living.

It's hard too, when there are so many shooting
acts around these days. Annie's always been
different. I guess that's what makes her stand out.

Other lady sharp-shooters dress up all fancy, but
Annie dresses real neat and simple. She does all
her own sewing, making her clothes, and
decorating her dresses and blouses with coloured
ribbon and pretty stitching. She ain't nothing like
folks imagine when they think of the Wild West –
not till she picks up her guns, that is.

Other shooters, men and women, don't always
shoot fair either. They cheat and, because folks
know they cheat, some think Annie cheats too,
which ain't right at all.

Frank told me the story of a faker he knew. This son-of-a-gun played a tune on a piano by shooting disks hanging from each piano key. That looked and sounded pretty smart until, halfway through the act, his gun jammed and he couldn't shoot any more. The trouble was, the piano tune kept on playing! Down in the orchestra pit, his accomplice hadn't seen what had happened and kept on thumping out the notes.

I ain't never been to Chicago, so I can't wait till the train pulls in tomorrow! Chicago has a special place in the story of Buffalo Bill's Wild West, because that's where Buffalo Bill got his first taste of stardom, back in December 1872.

At that time he wasn't called Buffalo Bill. He was plain William F. Cody, buffalo hunter, army scout, hero of the Indian wars and soon-to-be actor. He'd never acted in a theatre before and everyone could tell the only stage he'd ever been on was the overland stage out west.

But I guess the truth is, he didn't need to be an actor. He was the real thing from the time he started working as a rider, carrying mail for the Pony Express, when he was just fourteen years old. Then the Kansas Pacific Railroad offered him $500 a month to supply twelve buffalo a day, to feed the 1,200 men laying the new railroad track across the Kansas prairie. In eight months, Cody killed 4,280 buffalo and got the name Buffalo Bill.

It wasn't just buffalo he killed. In July 1876, when he was an army scout, he fought an Indian warrior called Yellow Hair single-handed, shot him dead and took his scalp. On top of all this, Buffalo Bill could shoot anything that moved. No wonder he was a showbiz hit from day one.

Buffalo Bill's Wild West has been going since July 1883, and this summer, folks can't get enough of it. Here's hoping they like it as much in Chicago.

25 MAY 1885 – CHICAGO

Yep – Chicago loves Buffalo Bill's Wild West!
And Chicago loves Annie Oakley.

   The papers say that 40,000 people came to the
show yesterday. That's one person in twenty in
the whole of Chicago. Good business in anyone's
book.

They cheer right from the start as the big canvas
curtain at the far end opens and a band of real
Indians in full warpaint gallop into the open-air
arena, yelling war cries. After them come the
cowboys, whooping and waving their Stetson
hats, then the Mexican cowhands waving their
sombreros.

Buffalo Bill gallops in on a big grey horse to the sound of trumpets from the Cowboy Band. He stops and salutes the audience packed into the horseshoe-shaped stands. Then he calls "Are you ready? Go!", which sends all the riders galloping round and round the arena, whooping and firing guns in the air. That gets the crowds going every time.

Annie comes on midway through the show, after the riding of the Pony Express and Buffalo Bill's re-enacted fight with Yellow Hair. She don't just walk into the arena – she skips in from the grandstand gangway, waving, bowing and blowing kisses. After the rough men of the Wild West, she sure is a change.

Out in the centre of the arena, Frank has all her rifles, shotguns and revolvers loaded and laid out on a wooden table covered with a silk cloth. He loads and fires the clay pigeons from spring traps and reloads Annie's guns during the act.

Annie don't miss too often. In fact, she tells me that sometimes she misses on purpose, to prove that the targets don't just explode on their own. One day I counted fifty-five hits out of the fifty-six glass balls Frank tossed in the air for her, and she only missed one because she tripped as she pulled the trigger.

She's shoots so fast too – and with both hands. I've seen her hitting targets holding the gun over her head and lying on her back across a chair. She can hit glass balls tied to the end of a rope Frank spins round his head. She can even toss two glass balls high in the air herself, then pick up a rifle, shoot the first ball, spin round and shoot the second before it hits the ground.

The audience's favourite stunt is Annie's mirror trick. In this, she turns her back on the target, takes aim with the rifle over her shoulder using a polished knife blade as a mirror, and still manages to hit the target. Sometimes she'll even jump the table after Frank has let fly a clay pigeon, run ten yards to pick up her gun and still hit the target before it lands. That's pretty snappy shooting, seeing that from start to finish the clay's only in the air for four or five seconds!

12 JUNE 1885 – BUFFALO, NEW YORK STATE

I don't know. That Annie! She seems to spring surprises as easy as she springs clays from a trap.

I guess I should have expected something to happen to Buffalo Bill's Wild West, seeing that we're here in the town of Buffalo. A special supper of buffalo tongue, or perhaps a buffalo hide for Buffalo Bill?

But when I saw who Major Burke, the publicity manager, brought into town today, I thought my eyes were playing tricks. Down the steps from the railroad car came the great Sioux warrior, Chief Sitting Bull himself! Some folks claim he's the one who killed General Custer at the famous battle of Little Bighorn nine years ago.

Major Burke says Sitting Bull's going to be touring with the Wild West this summer. You can't blame the major for looking mighty pleased with himself for getting a famous Indian chief like Sitting Bull to join the show. I'd say Major Burke is sitting pretty.

Sitting Bull watched the performance this afternoon from a carriage. As each act finished, the cowboys and Indians were introduced to him.

He only speaks in the Sioux language, but the major's hired an interpreter to translate for him. Maybe he can translate some of the things the cowboys say. There's some who could be talking foreign languages for all the sense they make.

Howdy y'all pardn'rs, yeehah!

Sitting Bull don't say too much, even in his own language. But when Annie came to greet him, the old chief looked mighty pleased. Would you believe it? Annie already knows him. Don't ask me how.

The major beckoned Annie over to introduce her to Sitting Bull, but she started talking to him like an old friend. It seems she had sent Sitting Bull a red silk handkerchief and some coins, and she wanted to check that they'd reached him way out west, at his home at Standing Rock. Can you beat it? Out of all the Indians and cowboys and frontier folk in the Wild West, the one person who knows Sitting Bull is little Annie Oakley!

30 JULY 1885 – Boston

We pulled into town three days ago, and the show's been a sell-out every performance. Mr Salsbury is telling the newspapers we could play here for two weeks and still be turning people away.

Mr Salsbury, Buffalo Bill and Major Burke are real smart when it comes to dealing with newspaper reporters. A whole bunch of them

were looking round the camp today, peering inside the Indian wigwams, watching the buffalo grazing and admiring the great long horns on the rodeo cattle, when the dee-licious smell of roast meat drew them to a big tent. Inside there were cowboys turning huge joints of beef over a camp fire.

Buffalo Bill asked the reporters to grab a place on the wooden bench and join in the "frontier barbecue" – and they didn't need no second invitation. Of course, not many folks on the frontier eat prime meat like this too often.

They're lucky to get a plate of beans and coffee, but how were those city slickers to know that? They stuck sharpened sticks into juicy ribs of beef and gobbled them down using their fingers. And boy, were they in a mess by the time they'd finished!

Still, they didn't seem to mind. And they wrote some real nice things in the newspapers about the hospitality you find on the frontier.

Good, free publicity – you can't beat it.

2 AUGUST 1885 – Boston

Mr Salsbury is always coming up with something
new. Here in Boston we're performing the Wild
West at night for the very first time. All around
the arena, huge flares light up the night sky. Frank
wasn't too happy about these at first – he thought
the artificial light might make it difficult for Annie
to hit her targets. But practising in the light of the
flares, Annie didn't miss a single shot. Frank told
her he guessed she could do it even in the dark.

At night the show looks real dramatic, but Mr
Salsbury was worried that some folks watching
might be scared of the loud bangs. So he put
Annie on at the start, right after the opening
gallop. And it works like a treat. Everyone is so
surprised to see a little girl all alone and shooting
targets that they don't take long to get used to the
sound of gunfire. Annie looks kind of gentle and
friendly, even when she's blasting away with her
shotguns. She gets folks used to the sound of
shooting and the rest of the show goes just fine.

2 SEPTEMBER 1885 – London, Canada

Not London, England, but a pretty jumpin' joint all the same!

Old Sitting Bull may be quiet, like most Indians, but he ain't dumb. Since he joined the Wild West, he's been making a tidy sum selling folks his autograph and pictures of himself. On top of the $50 he gets paid each week, he has a queue of people waiting to pay him a dollar a time for his signature or a picture.

Across the border, here in Canada, folks welcome Sitting Bull like a kind of hero. That's because he and his people escaped north to Canada and lay low for a while after General Custer and his men were all killed at Little Bighorn. He's met a whole lot of Canadian Indian chiefs. All the top people in big cities like Montreal have come to welcome him too. And he's had a whole lot more photographs taken, to turn into pictures to sell. By the time he goes home in a few weeks, he'll have plenty of money for his people back on the reservation.

II OCTOBER 1885 – St Louis, Missouri

Well, that's it for another season. Today was the last Wild West show of 1885. Tomorrow we all head for home until next year.

Sitting Bull has been looking at the sky for the last few days. He says it will be a cold winter. Will he be joining the show next year? I don't think so. "The wigwam is a better place for the red man," he told reporters. "He is sick of the houses, and the noises, and the multitudes of men."

It sounds to me like he'll be staying at home on the reservation, with his family from now on.

Annie's going to miss him, that's for sure. These last weeks she and the old chief have become even more friendly than they were before. Sitting Bull likes her shooting so much he's given her the name Little Sure Shot, and they say he's even adopted her into the Sioux nation as his daughter.

Tonight we had an early supper in the cook tent. Mr Salsbury, who's usually as quiet as Sitting Bull, made a short speech congratulating everyone on the most successful season ever. He told us that a million people had come to see the Wild West, and that we'd made a profit of $100,000. No wonder Buffalo Bill was smiling all evening. Back in March, the show was $60,000 in debt!

Nov Dec Jan Feb Mar Apr

29 MAY 1886 – ON THE TRAIN TO WASHINGTON D.C.

Sitting Bull was right – it was a cold winter. But that was months ago, and now everyone is looking forward to another successful season.

We all met up back in St Louis last month. The Wild West is bigger than ever, with twenty-six freshly painted railroad cars to carry the 240 performers, animal-handlers, canvasmen and loaders, plus all the animals and equipment.

There are new Indians and new cowboys this season, too. Sitting Bull is staying at home, as I guessed he would. In his place we've been joined by American Horse and Rocky Bear. I must be real careful to get their names right. They look mighty fierce and I don't think they'd take it too kindly if I called them Rocking Horse and American Bear by mistake.

Annie Oakley was such a success last season that Buffalo Bill's hired two cowgirls to appear in the show and another girl shooting star, Lillian Smith.

I don't know how Annie is going to like having a competitor. She don't mind Johnnie Baker, of course. He joined the show last year, same as Annie. Johnnie's a great shot like Annie; he can even shoot targets upside down standing on his head, but he's a young man. Lillian Smith's only a fifteen-year-old girl, and it ain't going to please Annie if she starts stealing her popularity. But she's a trier, our Little Sure Shot. I can almost hear her saying to herself, "Anything you can do, I can do better. I can do anything better than you."

I guess we'll know soon enough which of them is top gun. Tomorrow we open in Washington for a week. Then we're off to Philadelphia before going to New York for the rest of the summer.

26 JUNE 1886 – NEW YORK

New York! New York! It's my kind of town.

We only arrived at dawn today, and I love it already. New York is like a big juicy apple waiting to be gobbled up. To think that we're going to be here all summer! That's got to be better than moving from place to place every day or so.

The Wild West is going to be staged at a brand new arena on Staten Island. Across New York Bay you can see Manhattan, the richest part of the biggest, richest city in America. Folks there have machines that let them talk to each other down wires. They have this new-fangled stuff called electricity which brings them light down wires, too. I wonder how they tell which wire is which?

I hear that soon work will start on a new kind of building in Manhattan, which will be so tall folks are calling it a sky-scraper. They're naming it the Tower Building and it's going to stand eleven floors high. Imagine that! This here Tower Building ain't going to be a wooden building like the ones back west. It's going to have a framework made from big steel girders. That's how they can build it so high. If it works, I don't see why they couldn't use the same idea to build even higher buildings. If I came back in a hundred years' time, I guess I wouldn't recognize Manhattan. Why, there could be buildings twenty, perhaps thirty floors high. That really would be something to see!

4 JULY 1886 – New York

Independence Day, and what a crowd! Ferries brought thousands across the harbour to see us. The Wild West camp covers fifty acres of fields and woods, so to city folks it looks like their idea of the West itself. All day long, you meet them wandering round looking at everything. It's like we've come from another world, which I guess we have in a way.

They like watching the horses and the buffalo and the longhorn cattle. But it's the Indians living in the woods they really want to see. Their camp is just the same as any camp they have back home on the prairie. Visitors can't stop themselves patting the Indian ponies all tied up in line, peering inside the wigwams, or looking at the Indians as they sit round their fires, draped in blankets and smoking pipes. (What they don't know is that the Indians probably spend as much time playing white man's card games and gambling.)

On Sunday morning, folks in the Baptist church had a real surprise when some of the Indians turned up for the morning service and sat down in the front row. When the organ started to play "Nearer, My God, to Thee", they stood up and sang the whole hymn in the Sioux language. Some frontier preacher must have taught them, but they sure made an unusual choir.

The Indians like our food, too. Mr Salsbury treated them to a feast of "Yankee pies", which none of them had ever tried before. I don't know what was in them, but every Indian in camp tucked in. Five hundred pies had been eaten by the time they were fit to burst!

24 JULY 1886 – New York

Nearly 28,000 people came to see the show today.
There were so many we couldn't seat them all,
and now the carpenters are busy making more
seats. New York has never had an entertainment
this popular.

By now everyone has got used to performing
twice a day, even if the evening show does use
electric light. The pattern may be the same day
after day, but no one minds. There's always a
feeling of excitement as the stands begin to fill.
The cowboys rope and saddle their horses. The
Indians put on their warpaint. Stable hands hitch
the teams to the old stagecoach and the covered
wagons.

I help Frank load and prepare Annie's guns. When everyone's ready, Frank Richmond, the announcer, strides across the arena, climbs on to his raised platform in front of the mountain scenery, and opens the show in his booming voice: "Ladies and Gentlemen! Buffalo Bill and Nate Salsbury proudly present America's national entertainment, the one and only, genuine and authentic, unique and original, Wild West!"

That's the cue for the grand parade to gallop into the arena and for the 20,000 people all around to start cheering. Yep, it's true what Annie says. There's no business like show business.

24 SEPTEMBER 1886 – New York

There's just one more week to go before the show closes in Staten Island. The Wild West has made a heap of money this summer and still folks keep coming. Some have been so many times that they even know the names of all the horses and ponies.

Thanks to Major Burke, the newspapers have had something to write about the Wild West show every week. There can't be many people who don't know about the twin elks born in our camp,

or the wagonload of watermelons the Indians ate one afternoon, or the professor who arrived one day to prove that the Sioux people were descended from the Lost Tribes of Israel! Major Burke reckons any news is good news. That's sure been true this summer, there's no mistaking that.

It's been a good summer for Annie as well. Her shooting has made her famous all round New York and New Jersey. A lot of men who fancy themselves as sharp-shooters are feeling a mite nervous about this slip of a girl who breaks records with her gun as easy as she breaks glass balls.

Annie don't let this go to her head, mind. She never makes a big deal of her success. And if she does earn some extra money from giving shooting lessons, or winning competitions outside the show, she's always careful how she spends it. She's generous too. Why, only the other day she paid for fifty kids in the nearby orphanage to be her special guests at the show and afterwards at a slap-up "frontier feast" all of their own. When she was a youngster, Annie lived for a while in an orphanage, and she ain't never forgotten how it felt.

THANKSGIVING, 1886 – New York

Here we are, still in New York. The Indians are still camping out at Staten Island, only now the Wild West has moved indoors for the winter.

The summer show ended two months ago, back at the end of September. While we've had a break, our new winter show has moved into Madison Square Garden – a huge indoor arena which was once a railroad depot. This new show is a kind of play called "The Drama of Civilization – a Spectacle of Western Life and History". Most performers do pretty much what they did in the Wild West show, but we've got extra animals like moose, antelope and two trained bears to make it even more realistic.

Different scenes of the new show have their own huge backdrops, showing the prairies and the mountains of the west. Matt Morgan, the backdrop artist, had painted 15,000 square yards* of scenery by the time he finished. That's a lot of canvas and a lot of paint! And to make the show even more lifelike, there's a huge wind machine that blows leaves and brushwood across the arena in the scene showing a tornado.

* 12,541 square metres

PRAIRIE PAINT

We opened last night. 6,000 people were packed in to watch the new show, all dressed up like they were going to an opera. Annie's added a stunt on horseback to her shooting. She ties a handkerchief to her pony's pastern, just above the hoof, then unties it while she's galloping at full speed round the arena – and she does this riding *side-saddle*! No one, not even the cowboys and Mexicans, who've been riding since before they could walk, have ever seen anyone do this riding side-saddle. Just to prove how good she is on a horse, Annie can reach down from the saddle and pick a handkerchief off the ground. She can shoot targets while the horse jumps hurdles, or lying on her back as the horse gallops along.

4 DECEMBER 1886 – NEW YORK

I've got to hand it to Annie – she has the knack of making folks feel at ease, no matter who they are. Seeing that she is the adopted daughter of Sitting Bull, whose Sioux warriors killed General Custer and all his men, I wouldn't have expected the general's widow to take too kindly to her. But I couldn't have been more wrong. Mrs Custer thinks the world of Annie, and the two ladies are always together around Madison Square Garden.

"Custer's Last Stand", as it's called, has been added to the show this year. This is a battle scene in which Buck Taylor, King of the Cowboys, takes the part of General Custer and fights alongside his men at the Battle of Little Bighorn, until the Sioux warriors surround and kill them all. It's sad. It's heroic. The audience go crazy over it and Mrs Custer has been to see it several times.

Property of Sioux Indians
Trespassers will be scalped

I guess historians will argue and argue about what really happened at that battle on 25 June 1876, but no one can deny that the Sioux warriors had their greatest victory over the US army that day. I don't want to be unkind to the memory of General Custer, but it strikes me that he made some bad mistakes.

It's 2,000 miles from Madison Square Garden to the Little Bighorn, but every night the show brings that piece of American history alive right here in New York City.

12 DECEMBER 1886 – New York

Snow again today. The city looked real pretty. The Christmas decorations are all frosted white, and so are the trees and sidewalks. It must have reminded Annie of home, because she took it into her head she wanted to go on a sleigh ride, right here in the centre of New York! Once Annie has an idea, it's no use trying to stop her – even when her plans include driving a sleigh-pulling moose down Fifth Avenue.

Annie's got a way with animals, that's for sure. When she went to the stables this morning and led out Jerry, the moose which appears at the beginning of the show, Jerry followed as meek as a lamb. Annie hitched him to a sleigh, settled herself into the seat beside Frank, flicked the reins and headed Jerry off into the street.

New York ain't seen nothing like it. Folks out shopping just stood and stared as Jerry cantered by, and some looked like they'd seen Santa Claus himself getting in some practice for Christmas Eve.

Everything was going just dandy, till they rounded a corner and Jerry caught sight of a cart piled high with juicy, red apples. In two minutes that big old moose had eaten the lot, while the cart owner watched, dumbstruck. Frank managed to hand over $5 to cover the cost of the fruit before Jerry threw back his head, trumpeted and set off down the street to see what else he could find.

1 APRIL 1887 – AT SEA

It's going to be a short entry today, on account I don't feel so good.

Annie ain't the only little lady in the news right now. This year is Queen Victoria's Diamond Jubilee. She's ruled the world's biggest empire for fifty years, so we're sailing across the ocean to England to join in the celebrations and add to the fun.

I ain't never been to sea before, and even the old Deadwood stagecoach don't rock and sway like this ship. She's called the *State of Nebraska*, and one day out from New York the state of the passengers, let alone Nebraska or anywhere else in the Wild West, ain't too good. Indians, cowboys, Mexicans, mules, horses, stagehands, stable boys, even Colonel Cody (Major Burke got Buffalo Bill made a colonel specially for this trip to England) – we're all as sick as dogs.

If I didn't know better, I'd say Mr Salsbury planned for today to be our first full day at sea. Some April Fool joke, eh?

Oh, no... here I go again.

STATE OF
NEBRASKA

18 APRIL 1887 – LONDON, ENGLAND

Oh, boy! I never thought I be so glad to see a city again. Back in New York, the Indians were talking of a legend which says that any Indian who crosses the big water will fade away and die. After that voyage, I can understand what was spooking them.

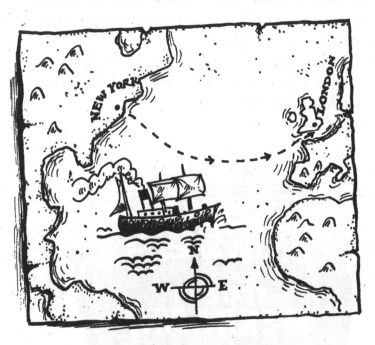

Still, we've made it. The New World has arrived in the Old World, and Major Burke has been busy letting London know. You can't go nowhere in this city without seeing posters and pictures of Buffalo Bill, Annie, Johnnie Baker, the Indians and the rest of the folks and animals in the show.

Londoners are real friendly, too. Since we arrived, we've been taken to restaurants and museums, to the opera and the theatre. One night the Indians sat in the front row of seats watching a famous English actor called Henry Irving. He was acting in a play by a famous German playwright, about a fellow called Faust who made some kind of bad deal with the devil. Don't ask me what they Indians made of it.

At the end, Henry Irving had Chief Red Shirt come up on stage to take a bow, along with Buffalo Bill, Annie and Frank, Mr Salsbury and Buck Taylor in all his cowboy gear. The audience clapped as loud for them as they did for the play. When Red Shirt asked what he thought of it, he answered pretty smart, saying it was "like a great dream".

28 APRIL 1887 – London

Preparations are almost complete for the grand opening! The Wild West is going to be part of the American Exhibition, showing all kinds of new machines and inventions from back home. Out in the west of London is a real grand-sounding place called Earl's Court, and that's where the exhibition and the Wild West are going to be all summer.

Although we don't open officially until 9 May, we put on a special show today for a man called Mr Gladstone and his wife. Mr Gladstone used to be Prime Minister in this country – that's like our president back home. They came for the day, looked round the Indian camp, and had lunch in the cook tent. Then, while Mrs Gladstone visited Annie in her tent, Mr Gladstone had a cigar with Buffalo Bill, Mr Salsbury and Chief Red Shirt.

6 MAY 1887 – London

A right royal day. This morning a line of gleaming carriages pulled up at the entrance to the American Exhibition, unlike any other coaches or carriages I'd seen before.

Word spread through the camp like a prairie fire that Edward Prince of Wales, the man who will be king after Queen Victoria, had come to see the show for himself! Seems he was so impatient, he couldn't wait any longer.

Prince Edward didn't spend too long looking round the exhibition. He made it mighty clear it was the Wild West he wanted to see. By the time Buffalo Bill showed him and the royal party to the royal box, they was chatting like old friends. The Prince is real keen on horses and hunting, and from the moment the Indians galloped in at he start of the show, he was on his feet, leaning forward and as excited as anyone who's ever seen Buffalo Bill's Wild West.

Prince Edward was on his feet for darn near the whole show. And when the old Deadwood stage rocked out of the arena with the last rattle of gunfire, he asked Buffalo Bill to present the "actors" to him.

"Your Royal Highness – Chief Little Bull... Chief Red Shirt... Buck Taylor... Mustang Jack ..." One by one, the stars of the Wild West were called forward to shake the future king and emperor by the hand. Annie was the only one who was different.

When Buffalo Bill announced, "Miss Annie Oakley", she stepped forward and shook hands with Prince Edward's wife, Princess Alexandra, *first*. Now that ain't something you do to a crowned prince, leastways not in this country!

Everyone says Princess Alexandra is a mighty sweet lady, and she gave Annie such a friendly smile. It seems Annie feels kind of sorry for the princess – folks say that Prince Edward has lady friends, and Annie don't think that's right when he's a married man.

She's always polite, mind. "You'll have to excuse me, please," she told the prince, "because I'm an American and in America, ladies come first."

12 MAY 1887 – LONDON

Prince Edward must sure have enjoyed his visit to the Wild West, because his Ma showed up this afternoon to have a look round the showground for herself.

A visit by a queen empress is special in anyone's book, but I hear that Queen Victoria ain't been to no theatre show outside her home in Buckingham Palace for twenty-six years. That makes the Wild West extra special, I reckon.

She drove through the stables, saw the Indians ride by in the arena, and then asked to meet Buffalo Bill, Chief Red Shirt, some Indian women and the two shooting girls, Lillian Smith and Annie Oakley.

Annie made the prettiest of curtsies and walked up to the queen, who told her, "You are a very clever little girl." Seeing as how Queen Victoria ain't no giant herself, and seeing as how Annie is a married woman, that seemed a strange thing to say, but Annie don't mind two bits. All she said was, she reckoned her costume made her look like she was shooting straight from high school, and left it at that.

II JUNE 1887 – London

Annie don't have no trouble convincing the
London crowds that she's about as good as you
can find when it comes to shooting. It ain't so
easy, though, with the top gun clubs. They ain't
used to seeing a woman shooting, and they sure
ain't used to a woman who can shoot better than
them.

The best club is the London Gun Club, on
Notting Hill. That's where Annie was invited to
give a private show today in front of the members
and their guests – people who know good
shooting when they see it.

Annie put together a routine which included
most of the shooting stunts she does in the Wild
West show.

* Don't forget to load guns!

- Throw balls in the air and shoot them ✓
- Break six balls in the air in four seconds ✓
- Break five balls in five seconds, the first
  with a rifle, the others with shotguns ✓
- Change guns three times ✓

Annie ran through the programme without a hitch, and afterwards she received a special gold medal as a souvenir of her visit.

Now Annie's accepted as a top gun among even the highest class of British shooters.

20 JUNE 1887 – WINDSOR CASTLE, ENGLAND

Today the whole Wild West show took the train to Windsor, to bring the prairie to the palace by putting on a special performance for Queen Victoria and her family and guests. It's fifty years since she was crowned – imagine that!

We ain't never had so many royal people to see us before. Nor I guess has any other show in history.

After the grand entry at the start of the show, on came little Annie for her shooting act. She was followed by the cowboys driving the steers into the arena and showing their skills – rounding them up, lassoing them and wrestling them to the ground. Next came a bucking bronco, with a cowboy bouncing in the saddle like a rag doll. After that, a Sioux medicine man beat his drum while Frank Richmond translated the death song he was chanting. Then a Pony Express rider raced round the arena, showing how the mail was first delivered out west, and after he'd galloped out, General Custer again made his "last stand".

When the time came for the Deadwood stage to roll over the prairie, Prince Edward asked if he could ride inside with the four kings. Old Utah Frank, the driver, ain't never had a group of passengers like them before.

The "Attack on the Deadwood Stage" is a big favourite with audiences, but I wonder how many know that what they see ain't that different to a *real* attack on a *real* stagecoach? Before the railroad was built, stagecoaches were the only way

most folks could make the long journey through the mountains and prairies out west. Indians and outlaws used to attack stagecoaches and rob their passengers, and it's a real Indian attack on a Cheyenne and Black Hills stagecoach which is acted out in the show.

So that's what the four kings and the prince found themselves in the middle of, as Utah Frank drove his mules round the arena while the Indians rode beside it, shooting and climbing aboard.

22 JUNE 1887 – London

Prince Edward is helping to make Annie even more popular with folks in London and all over this country.

One of the royal guests at the show we did at Windsor Castle was Grand Duke Michael of Russia, who fancies himself a good shot. He fancies himself in other ways too – I hear he's in England hoping to marry one of Queen Victoria's granddaughters, and the British people don't take too kindly to that idea. Now that Prince Edward and Buffalo Bill are such good pals, the prince suggested that Annie should have a shooting match against the grand duke. So they did and Annie won. She hit forty-seven out of her fifty targets, while Grand Duke Michael could only manage a score of thirty-six.

Well, to read the newspapers, you'd think Annie had saved the British Empire all by herself. They say the grand duke will be going home soon, empty handed, and they're congratulating Annie for that.

20 JULY 1887 – LONDON

Annie went to a place called Wimbledon today. This is where the champions show up every year for the top competition held in this country. The prizes are mighty impressive too, as much as £14,000.

Lillian Smith went along yesterday, but she didn't do too well. In fact she did real rotten. The clothes she wore didn't impress folks either.

With Annie it was different, even though the sport at Wimbledon ain't what she's used to. At Wimbledon everyone uses rifles. That's why Lillian fancied her chances. In the show she's billed as the rifle expert, while Annie's queen of the shotgun. Even so, Annie made a fairly good score, far and away better than Lillian's. To cap it all, Prince Edward happened to be watching, and made his way through the crowd to offer her his congratulations.

Annie ain't said too much about Lillian, but I know she's been worried since she arrived in the show. I guess she can sleep easier tonight, knowing she's proved once and for all that she's a better shot than Lillian with either a rifle or a shotgun.

I kind of wish Buffalo Bill had tried his hand at the Wimbledon championship too. Although we all know what a good shot he is, some English folk are saying he ain't as good as Annie and don't want to show himself up in public. I've noticed these last months that all the nice

things written about Annie in the newspapers and all her invitations to give shooting exhibitions are getting on Buffalo Bill's nerves. If I didn't know better, I'd say he's becoming jealous of her success.

31 AUGUST 1887 – LONDON

If I were Frank Butler, I guess I might be feeling a bit on the jealous side this summer as well. Frank don't make any big show of being Annie's husband. In fact, he stays in the background so much most folks don't even realize that Annie has a husband. That may be good for Annie's popularity, but it sure causes problems when Annie receives offers of marriage. A French count has kissed her hand and asked her to marry him. An English sportsman wanted her to marry him and run his country estate. Another young

Englishman sailed to Africa when he found out Annie was married. And a man in Wales sent a very serious proposal with a very serious picture of himself. Annie set this up as a target and put six bullets through it before sending it back with the message "respectfully declined".

Frank's sure going to be busy keeping more would-be Mr Oakleys away.

31 OCTOBER 1887 – LONDON (FOR THE LAST TIME THIS YEAR)

The Wild West played its last stand in Earl's Court today. Tomorrow we start taking down the wooden mountains and loading everything on to the railroad cars. This winter we're playing indoors in a big arena up north in Manchester.

I say "we". That ain't strictly correct. Just as I feared, things have got so bad between Annie and Buffalo Bill that she and Frank ain't coming with us. In spite of all her success this summer, they're quitting Buffalo Bill's Wild West, which leaves me with some tough thinking to do.

20 DECEMBER 1887 – NEW YORK

It ain't been an easy decision, but in the end I guess I was feeling homesick, so I came home with Annie and Frank and left the Wild West back in England.

Frank's got all kinds of ideas for making money. He plans to put Annie in a play called "Little Sure Shot, the Pony Express Rider" – as soon as he finds someone rich enough to pay for it.

In the meantime, he reckons Annie can pick up $200 a time from shooting matches. The first one will be in the middle of next month, against the English champion shooter, William Graham. Mr Graham is touring America, appearing in shooting matches against the top guns. So far, he ain't been beat.

22 FEBRUARY 1888 – EASTON, PENNSYLVANIA

Today was the third shooting match between Annie and William Graham. They'd won one match each, and the betting was against Annie when they took their marks on the snowy shooting field.

The bets may have gone against Annie because she insisted on taking Room 13 in the hotel. It's the same room she and Frank stayed in for the second match three weeks ago. Even though she won that, folks think she's chancing her luck taking a room with such an unlucky number. Not for the first time, she proved them wrong – by beating Graham forty-seven to forty-five.

Now she's beaten one of the best shooters in the world, Frank's lined up a whole lot more matches this spring. That should keep the money rolling in. So much for superstition!

2 APRIL 1888 – PHILADELPHIA

Annie went back on the stage today, and she ain't lost none of her old touch.

She's part of the touring show put together by Mr Tony Pastor. I thought he sounded like some kind of preacher, but I was wrong.

It turns out that Mr Pastor is just a regular showbiz manager, who provides good, clean family entertainment. Annie's act fits in just fine. Hers is the last act, the one the audience have been waiting to see, and the posters call her "the wonder of both continents... the greatest rifle and wing shot in the world".

24 MAY 1888 – PHILADELPHIA

Looks like Annie and Frank just had a near miss on a business deal. Frank's been busy looking for work, and he thought he'd found something real good when he came across a new Wild West show. The money looked real good too, and because Frank knew that the rich man paying for it had a fine reputation in business, he signed Annie up there and then – for $300 a week.

The trouble was, Frank didn't look at the other acts in the show first. When he did see them, he realized that he'd made a big mistake. A string of scraggy ponies and a few unhappy-looking Indians was as close as this show came to the Wild West. Worst of all were the so-called cowboys. One look at them and Frank could tell they knew as much about working the range as he knew about the moon!

OK, they wore the same clothes as cowboys do – a big hat to keep off the sun, a neckerchief to tie round their face in dust storms, leather covers (called chaps) to protect their legs and pants*, tall boots and a six-gun in a fancy holster – but, as Frank says, looks ain't everything.

"Any of you guys been to Abilene?" he asked. They just looked blank and didn't answer.

Now Abilene, as anyone out west will tell you, is one of the most important cattle towns there is. It was the first cattle town as well, from the time of the first big cattle drive in 1867. Texas cattlemen used to hire cowboys to drive the cattle 1,000 miles north to Abilene. Then they could be sent by railroad to the cities back east, where cattle were worth ten times the price they fetched in Texas. There ain't no cowboy worth the name who ain't heard of Abilene.

* Not underpants, stupid – trousers!

No wonder Frank had his doubts about these fellas in the show.

Of course, things today ain't like they were twenty years ago. Cattle don't get driven on long trails from Texas like they used to be. Nowadays, cowboys spend their time mending fences and rounding up cattle on big ranches. But this don't make no difference to how good they are at their work. That was another thing which worried Frank. These so-called cowboys could hardly sit in a saddle, never mind gallop after a steer, throw a lasso over its head and wrestle it to the ground.

He tried another cowboy question, but the answer was real dumb.

Buffalo Bill's Wild West had some of the best buckaroos in the whole country: cowboys who could stay sitting on the back of wild horse as it bucked and jumped around trying to shake him off. Frank also knew from the Mexicans working with Buffalo Bill that "buckaroo" comes from the Spanish word for cowboy, *vaquero*. Still, it was a pretty funny answer.

Frank gave them one last chance. "Say, can you fellas tell me where to find the chuck wagon?" That's where you get the food, between you and me.

Well, the answers he got had Frank near laughing his head off. One "cowboy" pointed him to the sick tent, and another one said he'd find it hitched up behind the steam engine on the railroad track.

Abilene, buckaroo and chuck wagon – the "cowboys" in this Wild West show didn't know ABC about real cowboy life, and I can see why that worried Frank. He don't want Annie getting mixed up in no cowboy outfit like that.

2 JULY 1888 – GLOUCESTER BEACH, NEW JERSEY

Boy, this has been a busy three months!

Back in April, Annie was starting out on the stage once again. Then it looked like Frank had got her tied up with that dud show. Now she's starting in a real good one. Not Buffalo Bill's, of course. His show has come back from Europe, but Annie still ain't part of that. This new show is run by a guy named Pawnee Bill, on account of the fact that he speaks the language of the Pawnee Indians as well as he speaks English.

Pawnee Bill's not his real name of course, just like Buffalo Bill ain't Mr Cody's. Pawnee Bill is really Gordon W. Lillie, but his show, like Buffalo Bill's, is real enough. In fact Pawnee Bill travelled for a time with Buffalo Bill, acting as interpreter for the Indians. He started his own show this year with 165 horses and mules, eighty-five Indians, fifty riders, and thirty trappers, hunters and scouts. They left him with a lot of mouths to feed and some mighty big railroad bills.

It was only thanks to Frank that Pawnee Bill was able to keep the show on the road. Frank read in a newspaper that Pawnee Bill had run out of money in Pittsburgh, and he told the rich man backing the show with the fake cowboys that Pawnee Bill's show was a much better bet. So Pawnee Bill got the money he needed to stay in business, and Frank got Annie out of a fix and into a show that could really go places. So here we are in New Jersey starting the

summer season with two performances a day. Yep, this show could run and run.

8 AUGUST 1888 – TROY, NEW YORK

"There is but one Annie Oakley and she is with us" – that's what the posters say for Pawnee Bill's Historical Wild West Exhibition and Indian Encampment. But it seems that by the time they got the name of the show sorted out and posters printed, they were already out of date. A month after joining, Annie was on the move again. Frank's got her another job in the theatre with Mr Pastor.

31 DECEMBER 1888 – PHILADELPHIA

It kind of feels like we're right back where we were last year. Frank finally found someone to pay for his stage play, and Annie opened as the star of "Deadwood Dick, or the Sunbeam of the Sierras" on Christmas Eve.

Even I can see that it ain't the greatest play ever written. It wasn't made any easier when the leading man walked out and never came back. That was the night before the show was going to open, so Annie and the rest of the actors had to make a lot of changes at the last minute. It didn't improve it none.

31 JANUARY 1889 – CHAMBERSBURG, PENNSYLVANIA

Deadwood Dick is dead and buried, and I don't think Annie is that sorry about it. The show hasn't been the smash hit Frank was hoping for, and last night it ran out of money. It would be more accurate to say that the money ran out of the show – the assistant manager sneaked out of the theatre taking all the ticket money with him, leaving everyone broke.

Frank don't seem too down that Annie's stage career has only lasted four weeks, because the New Year has brought some real good news for all of us. It seems that Buffalo Bill, Frank and

Annie have patched up the trouble that caused the split between them. Now he and Mr Salsbury are mighty keen to have Annie back in the Wild West once again. So we'll be back with our friends for the new season, and this year we're going back to Europe!

Buffalo Bill's Wild West European Tour
1889 - 90

Berlin
Munich
Paris
Banfelt
Rome
Barcelona

N
W - E
S

12 MAY 1889 – PARIS, FRANCE

I like Paris in the springtime! In fact I could get to
like Paris all year round, though I guess I'd like it
just that little bit more if I could understand what
folks here say and if *they* could understand *me*.

The whole of France is celebrating this year.
One hundred years ago the French Revolution
brought in a new way of governing the
country without kings and queens
and emperors, just like we did
back home after we beat the
British in the American
Revolution.

Here in the French capital
they're holding the Paris
Universal Exposition, and
they've built a huge metal tower
designed by a guy called
Gustave Eiffel. This is 320
metres high (as they say in
France) – that's 985 feet high
to folks like me – which
makes it far and away the
tallest building on earth.
Best of all, you can take a
seven-minute ride right to
the top in a kind of cage,
and that's been designed
by an American.

I got to hand it to this Eiffel guy. He's real smart when it comes to making things out of big metal girders. Why, he designed the framework inside the Statue of Liberty back in New York harbour. We used to sail past it when the Wild West was in Staten Island four years ago, and it was officially opened the November we played Madison Square Garden.

We're going to be here for the whole summer, like we were in London. I don't know if business is going to be as good as it was then, though. French folks don't know too much about the Wild West. They ain't read too much about it neither, seeing as how they speak French and folks out west speak English.

15 MAY 1889 – PARIS

Our first dress rehearsal showed the kind of trouble we might have getting through to the French. A good few thousand of the most important people in Paris, including the president and his wife, came to watch that afternoon. And they sat watching as dumb as clay pigeons when the show started.

The grand parade at the start of the show was the quietest I can remember. When the Deadwood stage rumbled on, the spectators didn't understand why it is so important in the history of the American West. Even the Indians charging in to attack it didn't mean anything to them. Mr Salsbury was watching at the entrance to the arena, and he looked mighty worried. Annie was next on and I saw him having a word in her ear.

Two riders cantered ahead and leapt from their ponies to hold up her targets. Annie ran in like she always does and bowed to the stands. Still there was silence. She started shooting with a pistol and a rifle. Targets shattered and the spectators started to stir. Next she shot the flames from a revolving wheel of candles.

You could tell all eyes were on her now as she broke two targets with one shot from her shotgun. Four targets followed, smashed with two shots. Up flew four disks, Annie shot two, grabbed a new gun, spun round twice and blasted the other pair into smithereens. Then, from the target line, she tossed two glass balls high in the air, ran back and jumped over the table, seized a gun, swung it round and hit the two balls while they were falling.

French folks may not understand the Wild West yet, but they understand shooting. As Annie tossed her last smoking gun on the table, roars and cheers rose from the stands, followed by a hail of handkerchiefs and parasols.

Mr Salsbury sent Annie right back on for her riding act. Astride her spotted pony, she dropped her hat on the ground and then picked it up at a gallop. Sliding head-down from the saddle, she tied her handkerchief round the pony's flying pastern. She grabbed a pistol from the grass and smashed six glass balls tossed in the air by another rider. Annie may say "You can't win a man with a gun", but that day she sure won over the whole of Paris. Now, folks could see what makes the Wild West so special.

10 JUNE 1889 – PARIS

That clever inventor, Mr Edison, has brought his latest invention over from America. It's the most popular thing at this exhibition, apart from the Eiffel Tower. Though I'm mighty pleased that the Wild West comes a close third!

What Mr Edison has come up with is a machine that stores sounds and then lets folks listen to them. Every morning long queues are waiting for his stand to open, so folks can take it in turn to put kind of cups over their ears to

listen to music or to other folks talking. It seems to me that Mr Edison could be on to a good thing. Who knows, some day we might be able to listen to all kinds of sounds on machines like his in our homes. Wouldn't that be something!

22 JULY 1889 – PARIS

Annie ain't letting her success go to her head. Now the show's all the rage in Paris, no one could blame her for taking things easy. But that ain't Annie and Frank's way. Ever since we got here, she's been practising a new pistol stunt.

Pistols ain't that accurate, as any cowboy will tell you. Most of them can't hit a target more than a few yards away. Annie can, though. In this new trick, she puts a bullet right through the ace of hearts on a playing card ten paces away. Then Frank holds the same card edgeways to her, and Annie slices it right through, edge to edge!

With shooting like this, it ain't hard to see why so many important people want Annie to shoot for them. Mr Carnot, the president of France, has told Annie that if she ever wants to give up showbusiness for a different kind of work, there's a job as an officer in the French army open to her any time. Not long ago, the King of Senegal, down on the west coast of Africa, asked if Annie would work for him back home. It seems Senegal has a whole load of wild animals which keep attacking and eating his people. Annie told them both that she is happy where she is right now, but she'd bear their offers in mind.

4 MARCH 1890 – Rome, Italy

It's been another bad winter for the Wild West, but spring's here once more and we're in Rome, so things are starting to look up!

After the show closed in Paris, we sailed to Spain, where we were supposed to appear in Barcelona. Barcelona's best forgotten, however. The Indians didn't like the place as soon as they saw the huge statue of Christopher Columbus. "It was a bad day for us when he discovered America," one of them complained.

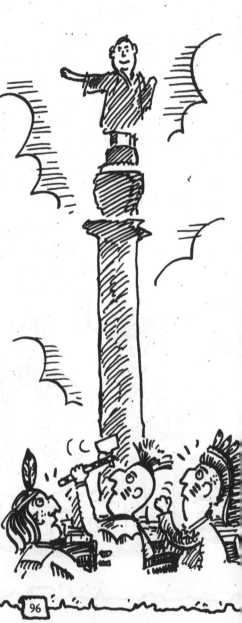

Then thousands of people in the city took sick. In camp, the Indians took sick, and ten of them died. Frank Richmond, the show's announcer, died. Barcelona was a real sad city, and we were glad to leave in January.

Today was like the Wild West should be – folks having a good time and seeing life on the prairie like it really is. An Italian nobleman called the Prince of Sermoneta had heard how skilled our cowboys are at taming wild horses. So he matched some of his best bucking broncos against them. No one in Europe could ride these horses, and the prince was real sure none of Buffalo Bill's cowboys could ride them either.

I guess the prince didn't understand bronco-busting back home. The word *bronco* means 'wild' in Spanish, and wild horses have been tamed out west for as long as Spanish settlers,

Mexicans and every other type of cowboy have been riding the range. You can't live and work on the prairie without riding a horse, but a wild horse has got to be controlled and taught to obey its rider. That's a dangerous business which needs a lot of skill and a lot of guts. It ain't for me, I don't mind admitting.

All cowboys out west learn skills that Mexican riders learned before them. They use lariats, ropes with special slip knots, to catch wild horses. Then the horses are tied to a "snubbing post" to hold them steady while a saddle or thick leather strap is fitted tightly round their flanks. Then a broncobuster gets on the horse, the horse is released and the cowboy holds on for dear life as the bronco bucks and leaps, trying to throw him off. Folks like watching this so much that bronco-busting is a big part of rodeo shows.

Well, Rome ain't used to rodeos, and it took several days to get everything ready. Strong fences had to be built to keep the horses away from the crowds. Today 20,000 turned up to watch, and 2,000 carriages were parked round the field.

When the time for the contest began, two of the prince's wildest horses were let into the arena, without saddle or bridle. They looked mighty mean, but Buffalo Bill announced that his cowboys would tame them, and he gave the signal to start them off. The horses bucked and jumped in all directions, and bent themselves into every kind of shape.

In spite of this, it only took the cowboys five minutes to catch the horses, saddle them, stop them bucking and ride them round the arena while the spectators clapped and cheered.

Buffalo Bill didn't get to keep those horses, but his cowboys showed the prince a thing or two about riding.

23 APRIL 1890 – MUNICH, GERMANY

We had a visit from another prince today. He also learned something about horses in the Wild West.

This was Prince Luitpold of Bavaria, who dropped in during a rehearsal. He was so impressed when he saw Annie shooting that he asked if she could shoot a coin he tossed in the air. Of course,

Annie can shoot coins as easy as most folks can spend them! The prince was admiring his coin with a hole in it, which I guess he won't be able to spend now, when Jim Mitchell, one of the cowboys, yelled out a warning cry.

LOOK OUT!

It seems that Dynamite (now, there's a good name for a bucking bronco) had escaped, and was charging straight at Annie and the prince! Annie saw the danger and, small as she is, she threw herself at the prince and pushed him to the ground, just in time for Dynamite to jump right over the two of them.

The Prince was mighty pleased, and sent Annie a beautiful diamond bracelet as a present. All she said was, "I suppose I am the only person alive that ever knocked a ruling sovereign down and got away with it."

23 AUGUST 1890 – BERLIN, GERMANY

My, how time races by! It seems like it was only yesterday we were sailing away from Barcelona, and now we've travelled all over Germany and are playing Berlin for a month.

All this travelling has kept the Wild West team busy, packing and loading, unpacking and unloading.

In most places folks don't take too much notice of this, but in Germany it seems like we can't drive in a tent peg without some German army officer watching and noting how the teamsters do it. We've had groups of officers taking notes on how we break camp, how we load the railcars with all the animals and gear, how we take everything off the trains, even how many men it takes to do each job. For some reason the German army can't get enough information about our camp kitchens. I reckon they've copied so many details and diagrams that if Germany ever goes to war, her army will be the best fed in Europe.

23 SEPTEMBER 1890 – ON THE TRAIN IN GERMANY (DON'T RIGHTLY KNOW WHERE)

Annie had another visit from a German prince a couple of days ago. He is Crown Prince Wilhelm, who's going to be Emperor of Germany one of these days. The Crown Prince had heard about Annie's stunt, the one where she shoots the ash from the end of a lighted cigarette in Frank's mouth.

Some fake shooters play tricks with this sort of stunt, and I guess the prince wanted to find out if Annie and Frank were faking it too. So he asked Annie to let him hold the cigarette while she shot away the ash.

Well, knocking a prince to the ground is one thing, but shooting at a prince could land a girl in a whole lot of trouble. Annie wasn't too keen on the idea. But Crown Prince Wilhelm insisted, and they agreed to let him hold the cigarette in his fingers. That way she wouldn't be firing the bullet just an inch or two from his head.

Annie ain't never missed with this stunt, and she didn't miss this time. The ash flew away and the crown prince could see that the trick weren't no fake. Of course, if Annie had missed, the history of Europe could have been a whole lot different in the years ahead.*

31 JANUARY 1891 – BANFELT, ALSACE (GERMANY)

This ain't been the start to the year anyone in the show was expecting. It don't feel right when a year begins with bad news.

News reached us from Buffalo Bill and Major Burke, who are back home this winter while the rest of the show is holed up in this old castle in Germany. From what they tell us, it seems like there was some kind of uprising on Sitting Bull's reservation, way out at Standing Rock. Annie's kind of upset about her friend Sitting Bull, as you can imagine. Word reached the government in Washington D.C. that there was going to be trouble among the Indians, and Buffalo Bill and Major Burke were asked to travel out to meet Sitting Bull, to see if they could persuade him to stop the uprising. This was in late November last year.

* Crown Prince Wilhelm became the German Kaiser. Many people blamed him for starting the First World War in 1914.

I can see why the government thought Buffalo Bill might be able to win Sitting Bull round, after he had been in the Wild West and all. But I reckon he might not have been the best choice. With a name like Buffalo Bill, you ain't going to be popular with most Indians. It seems to me that a fellow who made his name from killing buffalo might have a hard time calming down a band of Indians on the warpath.

Hi, I'm I-didnt-really kill-all-your-Buffalo Bill.

Not many folks understand how important buffalo are to tribes like the Sioux. For thousands of years they have depended on buffalo for just about everything: food, shelter, clothing, blankets – the works. That's why they think the buffalo is sacred.

Sacred Buffalo Stores (SBS Inc)

meat — boots   glue (boiled buffalo hooves)
           fuel (dried buffalo chips – OK, poo)
moccasins   bowls (buffalo horns)
bedding
saddles   hoes (buffalo shoulder bones)
      cups (buffalo horns)   clothes
sled runners (buffalo ribs)
         tasty treats (buffalo tongue)
wigwams   thread (buffalo sinew)
bowstrings   fly swatters (buffalo tails)

You name it, we've got it, or we'll make it!

When the buffalo disappeared, the Indians' way of life disappeared with them, and white folks started taking over Indian lands. I guess that's why the tribes around Sitting Bull were real worked up.

In the end, Buffalo Bill never got to see Sitting Bull. A troop of Indians in the police force went to arrest him ten days before Christmas. At first, Sitting Bull seemed to be going with them quietly. But something went wrong. Someone started shooting, and as the bullets flew, Sitting Bull was gunned down.

Apparently Sitting Bull's followers joined forces with Chief Big Foot, and fought the US army at Wounded Knee, but they were defeated. They didn't fight no more after that. Instead, they went back to live on their reservations, and now there ain't nothing to stop white folks taking all the lands that once belonged to the Indians.

Buffalo Bill writes from home to say he'll be coming over to Europe this spring to begin a new season touring Buffalo Bill's Wild West around Europe. If it wasn't for him and the likes of Annie Oakley, no one would know what the real American Wild West was like. They won't find it back home no more, that's for sure.

THE REST OF THE STORY

Phil McCartridge, whose diary ends at this point, was right. Buffalo Bill's Wild West continued to thrill audiences in America and Europe with its real-life action for another twenty-two years. By that time, Buffalo Bill had been forced to sell most of the show to other businessmen. In 1908 he had teamed up with Pawnee Bill, but his money problems didn't get any better and Buffalo Bill's Wild West closed for the last time in September 1913.

Films had taken over from big outdoor shows by then. People were still eager to see cowboys and Indians, stage coaches and buffalo in action, but now they flocked to see western movies instead. Out in the west itself, new cattle ranches and huge farms had changed the way of life that the Indians had known only a hundred years earlier.

Annie Oakley continued to appear with Buffalo Bill until 1901, when she and Frank retired from public life. She carried on shooting, giving private exhibitions for another twenty years, until she retired for good in 1923. Only a short time afterwards, she was seriously injured in a car accident which left her weak and frail. She died at the beginning of November 1926. Frank followed her eighteen days later. They were buried together, back in Darke County, Ohio, where Annie had grown up and where the most famous woman shot in the world had fired a gun for the first time as a little girl.

Annie's fame lived on in the theatre, in the cinema and later on television. Twenty years after she died, she achieved Frank's theatrical dream in a way, when a musical based on her life story opened in New York. This was called "Annie Get Your Gun", and it became a big hit on Broadway, where it ran for three years before being turned into a film, which made over $4,650,000.

This way, the memory of Annie Oakley lived on, and for many years she continued to be as popular as she had been during her years of thrilling audiences in the dusty arena of Buffalo Bill's Wild West.

PUBLISHER'S ADDENDUM

Although it cannot be denied that many of the people, dates and events recorded in this book are real and correct, we have to confess to a few concerns, not unlike those Frank Butler had about the fake cowboys he met in 1888.

Annie Oakley kept a scrapbook and a diary for more than forty years, but nowhere in those can we find any mention of a personal stagehand, let alone one named Phil McCartridge.

Our concerns grew when we tried to contact the two so-called experts, who had flown to Europe at Mr Dickinson's expense to prove that the diary was genuine. No university directory in North America lists either Larfinstock College or Imina State University. We did find over 50,000 men named Joe King, however. So far, six have answered our enquiries and 597 have messages on their answerphones.

Attempts to trace Dr Rusty Brayne have been less successful. After a number of rude replies, our staff have stopped telephoning people listed as "R. Brayne" and asking, "Have you got a Rusty Brayne in your house?"

While the search continues, we have reluctantly concluded that both "experts" were probably fakes, and that Mr Dickinson was tricked into giving free European holidays to a couple of con-men.

Sadly, it looks as if Mr McCartridge is a fake as well. For a so-called stagehand to sharp-shooter Annie Oakley, his diary contains very little detail about guns and ammunition. Indeed, at the beginning of the diary, he gives the name of one make of gun as Double Gloucester.

Double Gloucester is, of course, a type of English cheese. It is now our opinion that the whole thing stinks.